leapfrog

Little Joe's
Big Race

First published in 2000
Franklin Watts
96 Leonard Street
London
EC2A 4XD

Franklin Watts Australia
45-51 Huntley Street
Alexandria
NSW 2015

A CIP catalogue record for this book is available
from the British Library.

ISBN 0 7496 3712 9 (hbk)
ISBN 0 7496 3832 X (pbk)

Series Editor: Louise John
Series Advisor: Dr Barrie Wade
Series Designer: Jason Anscomb

Printed in Hong Kong

For Verona – A.B

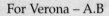

Little Joe's Big Race

by Andy Blackford

Illustrated by Tim Archbold

W
FRANKLIN WATTS
LONDON•SYDNEY

Little Joe didn't like
Sports Day.

He was so little, a frog could jump higher.

He was so slow, a tortoise
could run faster.

But Little Joe was good
at balancing things.

He decided to win
the egg and spoon race.

And Little Joe did win!

But he was so excited,
he forgot to stop.

He ran out of the school gates ...

... and through the town.

He ran all day ...

... and all night too.

He swam through rivers.

He ran up ...

... and down mountains.

One day, there was a loud CRACK!

Out of the egg popped
a chicken.

Still Joe kept running.

He ran through the sun ...

... and through the rain.

Soon, the chicken grew
too big for the spoon.

Little Joe had to carry
him on a spade.

At the same time,
Little Joe grew bigger
and bigger.

One year later, Little Joe arrived back at school.

It was Sports Day again.
Everyone was cheering.

"Well done, Big Joe!"
cried the teacher.

"You've won the chicken and spade race!"

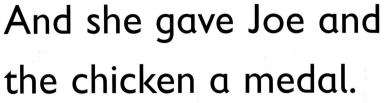

And she gave Joe and
the chicken a medal.

Leapfrog has been specially designed to fit the requirements of the National Literacy Strategy. It offers real books for beginning readers by top authors and illustrators.

There are 25 Leapfrog stories to choose from: